# The haunted Churchbell

written and illustrated by

## Barbara Ninde Byfield

DOUBLEDAY & COMPANY, INC., GARDEN CITY, NEW YORK

Library of Congress Catalog Card Number 72-137849.  Copyright © 1971 by Barbara Ninde Byfield. All Rights Reserved. Printed in the United States of America.

Late one dark and snowy afternoon some four hundred years ago Sir Roger de Rudisill, spurs jingling and teeth chattering, became lost in a blizzard on his way from one adventure to another. Spying a small stone hut ahead, he urged his horse forward.

"No one seems to be home," shivered Sir Roger to himself as he knocked loudly for the third time. "Dare I shelter here without asking? It looks snug and cozy...." But just then the blizzard lifted for a moment. Directly below, down the mountain, Sir Roger could see the small village he was looking for.

But fright and terror hung thick on the little village. "Upon my soul, Boniface," asked Sir Roger of the Innkeeper, "why this dire change in your pleasant village? Last month when I passed through, all was merry, hospitable, and cheerful. Now I see only barricades, bonfires, boarded-up windows! Furthermore, not a snowman in sight. Where are the children?"

'Ah, you do well to ask, Sir Roger," sighed the Innkeeper. "For a week now we've been in a state of siege, as you might say. You know us well, and there's not a coward or craven among us, but there's something ugly abroad in the night and I fear we'll come to grief if we've no help."

"It all started last week when the church-bell's rope broke," said the Butcher, coming out of his shop cautiously.

"And the same day, the belfry stairs, old and rotten as they were, collapsed," put in the Blacksmith, pointing toward the church.

"And until the Setxon comes back from the city with the new rope, we can't ring the bell," added the Baker, peering out of his window.

It's most troublesome, not having the bell," put in the Innkeeper as he led Sir Roger to the church. "You know how we rely on it. It's a peaceful bell, easy to wake to and not nagging, melodious at noonday, and soothing to put a child to bed by at night. Everything a bell should be."

"Yes indeed," replied Sir Roger, "a very fine bell, the best in these parts. But surely not having it ring for a week can't be the cause of all your trouble?"

"But it has been ringing for a week, that's just it! Not during the day, but at midnight, every night, just once!"

"I thought you said it couldn't?" questioned Sir Roger.

"That's just it! It can't! Yet it does! Without human hand to touch it. Sir Roger, that bell is HAUNTED!"

Leaving the freezing church, they all settled by the welcome fire in the inn. An old gaffer sitting in a corner continued the tale. "And worse still, we hear wolves in the mountains at night.

"In my granddaddy's time there were great famous wolf packs roaming the mountains, stealing away children, and killing our sheep something terrible. But the great winter of '02 froze them all, and there hasn't been a wolf nigh the village since. Until this week...ghost wolves, every night!" And at that moment down the mountain did indeed come a sound very like the painful and low howling of a hungry wolf.

"Now all week," said the Blacksmith, "we've set watches all around and about the church, in the graveyard, on the roof, and as close as mortal soul could get to the bell. Yet it still rings once and loud, with none to touch it, and the snow beneath and all around is always smooth too and undisturbed. Nor hand nor stick nor stone touches that bell, yet it rings. Sir Roger, we've come to the end of our rope."

"Hmmm…" mused Sir Roger, vastly intrigued with this mystery.

"Yes, yes?" they all asked eagerly, for his reputation as an adventurous spy was well known to them all.

"There's just a chance that something I saw earlier may be part of the answer. I'm not sure, and I make no promises, but if a handful of you stout fellows will come with me up the mountain this night, perhaps we can end this mystery."

So while the Butcher, Baker, and Blacksmith went to don their warmest wear and gather their weapons, Sir Roger bade the Innkeeper and his wife refill his tankard and put more of their excellent sausages in the pan. "For," as he said, "if I must needs double my journey this night, I'll do so on a full stomach at least. And could I trouble you for just one more of your famous pancakes, good lady?"

Well fed and wrapped warmly, the four started up the steep and snowy trail with the good wishes and prayers of the anxious villagers keeping them company.

The Innkeeper, true to his profession, placed a large roast on the spit and, calling for fresh loaves, cheeses, butter, and a fine old ham from his larder, proceeded to build up the fire and tap a new keg of ale against their safe return.

The howling of the wolf came closer and closer as Sir Roger and his men toiled up the mountain. Drawing nigh the stone hut he had stopped at earlier that day, he whispered "Shhhhh....Quiet it is, fellows. Hide yourselves, and wait for my signal."

Suddenly the howling stopped and the door of the hut was thrown open. Out strode the largest, fiercest man they had ever seen, gnashing his teeth in rage. Picking up an enormous handful of snow and ice, he packed it into a hard icy ball and pulled from beneath his fur robe a huge and sturdy slingshot.

"BONG!" went the churchbell far below.

"NOW!" roared Sir Roger, and down went the Hermit in a flurry of snow, ice, and fur.

"ZOUNDS!" cried the Blacksmith. "A snowball and sling-shot!"

"Of course," called the Baker. "Why didn't we think of that!"

"When it hit the bell it broke into snowflakes! No wonder there was no evidence!" said the Butcher.

"I thought it might be that," answered Sir Roger, "when I saw that huge slingshot hanging on the wall as I peered through your window this afternoon. And now, sir," he continued, "will you tell us why in the name of Beelzebub you've been frightening the village out of its wits?"

"And if you happen to keep wolves as pets?" asked the Baker fiercely. "The milk has fair curdled in the cows, we've been that frightened."

And to their amazement, the huge Hermit began to cry. With tears running into his beard, he led them into his hut and pointed to a most amazing object in the corner.

"It's my ch-ch-ch-cello!" he sniffled. "I never meant to frighten anyone. You see, I just finished making it myself last week, but the very day it was ready, you stopped ringing the church bell and I couldn't tune it. You know your bell sounds a perfect A? A very fine bell it is, and yet I had no way to tune the strings."

"Egad, a musical Hermit!" said Sir Roger.

"Not really," answered the Hermit modestly, bringing out his best bread and honey. "But you see, I've been rather lonely of late. No one comes up to see me, I suppose because I'm new in these parts and a bit large and strange to look at. People do seem to think Hermits like to be left alone, and so they do, most of the time, but not all the time. So I thought I'd make a cello and have a little music to keep me company, and perhaps if I learned to play something pretty, it might attract a visitor now and then."

"Well, you've certainly done that at least!" laughed Sir Roger, and everyone joined in, for it was now apparent that the Hermit was the jolliest of fellows and meant harm to none.

And as soon as he put bow to string, the howling of the "wolf" was solved as well, for the cello, being strung with knotted bits of wire, string, and hairs from the Hermit's beard, gave forth a large and mournful sound as rough and furry and lonely as the Hermit himself, very like a hungry wolf if you didn't know what it was.

Then they promised the Hermit that as soon as the Sexton brought back the new bell rope it would be rung thrice daily as before, and more on Sundays, which should help keep the cello nicely in tune. The Blacksmith promised to send up some extra-long horsehairs for the bow, and the Butcher said he would add some fine gut for new strings, which pleased the Hermit vastly.

Bidding the Hermit good night, they found their way down the mountain quickly, the good man having provided excellent torches and the loan of his toboggan, large enough for all, although a bit bumpy.

And the merry sounds of the cele-
bration that night floated up the
mountain so happily that the Hermit came down and joined them all
far into the night.

If there were some sleepyheads the next morning, they were still full of laughter at themselves for having been so frightened by a snowball, a cello, and a lonely Hermit.

BARBARA NINDE BYFIELD was born in Abilene, Texas. She attended the University of Wyoming and the Art Students League of New York. She has illustrated several children's books, including *Upright Hilda* and *The Giant Sandwich*, and is the author-illustrator of *The Eating in Bed Cookbook, The Glass Harmonica,* and *The Haunted Spy*. Mrs. Byfield lives with her two daughters, Barbery and Tamsen, in New York City.